# THE BEAR WHO STARED

## DUNCAN BEEDIE

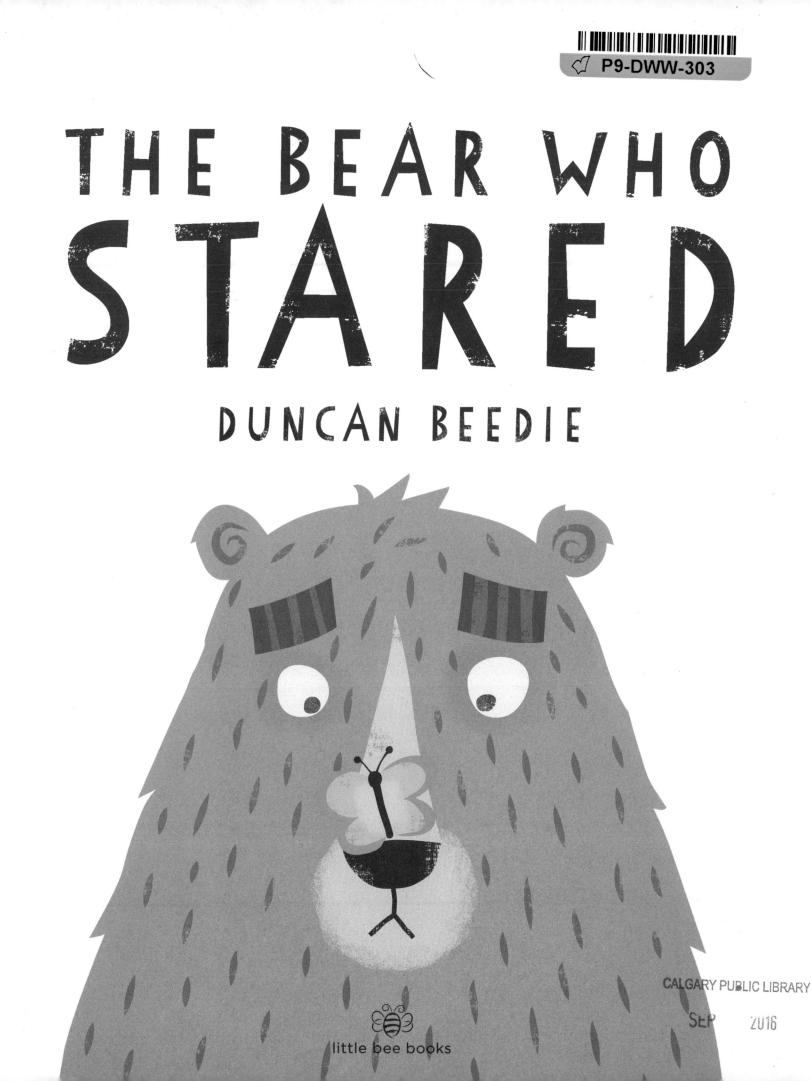

little bee books

There once was a bear who liked to **stare** . . .

and **stare** . . .

and . . .

stare.

Every day, Bear emerged from his cave and **stared** at everthing he saw.

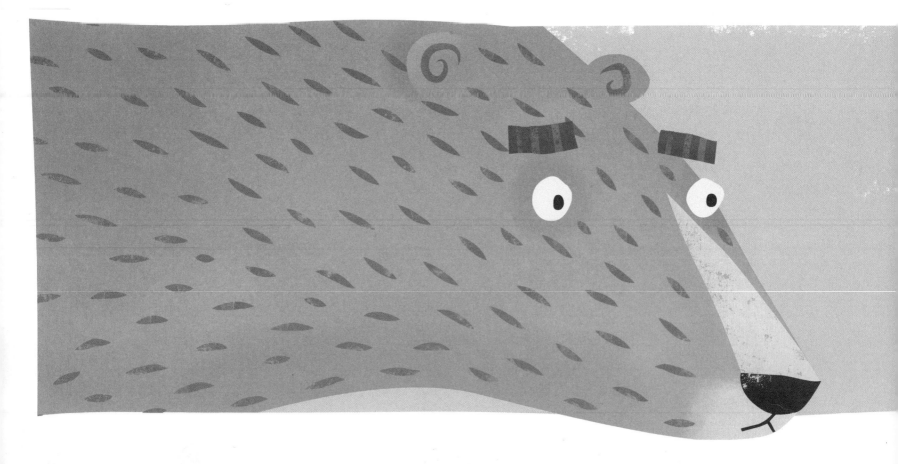

One morning, he **stared** at a family of ladybugs
who were having their breakfast on a small leaf.

"What are you **staring** at?" squeaked the daddy ladybug. "We're trying to have our breakfast in peace!"

And with that, they scuttled off to find somewhere else to eat.

Bear strolled farther into the forest
and climbed a big tree.

He **stared** at a bird feeding
her chicks in their nest.

"Can I help you?" asked the bird.
Bear did not answer. He just **stared.**

The chicks did not like Bear **staring** at them.

They didn't want him watching while they ate their lunch.

"Go on, *sshhhooooo*!" squawked the bird.

"Get down on the ground where you belong!"

Bear climbed back down to
the forest floor, where he spied
a badger's burrow.

He poked his head into the
entrance . . . and I'm sure you
can guess what happened next.

"Oi! Stop **gawking!**" barked the badger,
and he bit poor Bear on his nose.

(He was a particularly angry badger.)

Bear pulled his head from the badger's burrow with a
**POP!**

and skulked off, rubbing his sore nose.

Before long, Bear found a log to sit on
by a large, green pond.

He sat and pondered by the pond.

Bear didn't mean to annoy all the
other animals. He was just naturally curious
but too shy to say anything.

"I've seen that look before," said a small,
croaky voice coming from the pond.

Bear looked down and saw a plump little frog.
Bear **stared** at the frog.

The frog **stared** back with his big, googly eyes.

"Not much fun being **stared** at, is it?"
said the frog.

"I suppose not," muttered Bear. "It's just that I don't
know what to say to anyone, and before I've had a
chance to think, it's too late."

Bear **stared** into the water . . .
and saw another bear **staring** back at him
with the same wide, curious eyes.
He looked just like Bear in every way, but this bear
wobbled and was a strange green color.

Then something extraordinary happened.
The green bear blinked, and his mouth
turned into a **smile** . . .

. . . which turned into a big, **happy** grin.

"You see?" said the frog. "Sometimes a **smile** is all you need. I may have big, googly, **starey** eyes, but I also have the widest smile in the whole forest."

Then the frog showed Bear his biggest, widest, happiest **smile**, before diving into the water.

As the frog disappeared,
so did the wobbly, green bear.

The next day, Bear trudged out of his cave.
He saw the ladybug family enjoying their
breakfast on a small leaf.

The daddy ladybug was just about to gather
up their things and leave, when Bear said,
"Hello!" with a big **smile** on his face.

"Oh, hello!" replied the daddy ladybug,
and he **smiled** back.

Bear strolled happily off into the forest.

Bear made lots of new friends that day,
and he did not feel the need to **stare.**

Although . . .

. . . he did have one new friend who didn't mind Bear **staring** at him. . . .

And he was just as good at **staring** back.

For Avarin (our bear cub).

little bee books

An division of Bonnier Publishing
853 Broadway, New York, New York 10003
Copyright © 2015 by Duncan Beedie
First published in Great Britain by Templar Publishing.
This little bee books edition, 2016.

Manufactured in China 0080316
First Edition 2 4 6 8 10 9 7 5 3 1
Library of Congress Cataloging-in-Publication Data is available upon request.
ISBN 978-1-4998-0285-6
littlebeebooks.com
bonnierpublishing.com